MAGIC ROUNDABOUT
TIME FOR BED STORIES

Stories and Illustrations by
JOHN LEEDER

1595 6

THE PRIZE ROSE

MR. MACHENRY spent all morning in his garden busily removing the weeds growing round his beautiful blooms. He smiled to himself as he gazed around his lovely garden, which was filled with flowers of every type and colour. He had marigolds arranged in diamond shapes, lupins arranged in star shapes, and petunias arranged in ring patterns around the sunflowers and hollyhocks which grew tall against the wall of the garden. Mr. MacHenry loved all the flowers in his garden, but pride of place went to his roses, and people came from miles around just to look at the beautiful display. Mr. MacHenry was always delighted to give a rose to put in the buttonholes of all who came to look.

All the roses in the garden were beautiful, but the loveliest of all was not to be found in the garden, but in his greenhouse. You see, this was the very special rose he had grown for the Willow Warble Show.

"I think that you will win the first prize," said Dougal, as he popped his head over the garden wall.

"Nothing surer," Zebedee exclaimed, as he went springing from lawn to lawn.

The evening before the show Mr. MacHenry

trundled down the garden path to the greenhouse to give a little water to the bloom which everyone knew would be the finest in the show. He walked slowly to the bottom of his greenhouse only to find that his cherished rose had gone.

"Oh, dear me!" said Mr. MacHenry sadly. "It is the finest rose that I have ever grown, and now it has been stolen."

Not knowing what to do next, he walked slowly from the greenhouse, sadly wondering who could have taken his beautiful rose.

The following morning Mr. MacHenry was gloomily preparing his breakfast when there was a knock at the door and who should be there but Mr. Rusty. Mr. MacHenry could hardly believe his eyes when he saw what Mr. Rusty was carrying. Yes, it was his beautiful rose.

"I borrowed your rose to cheer up an old friend of mine who is ill in hospital," said Mr. Rusty. "You were asleep in the chair when I called yesterday evening and I didn't like to disturb you."

Mr. MacHenry was so happy he completely

forgot about his breakfast and he danced with glee at the sight of his treasured bloom.

"I must hurry to the Willow Warble showground before the judging begins," he said. And he picked up the rose and hurried down the lane to the show.

The judges all agreed that they had never seen such a fine bloom and had no option but to award Mr. MacHenry the first prize.

"You are the star of the show," said Mr. Rusty.

"You may give the rose to your friend in hospital," Mr. MacHenry told Mr. Rusty. "If it makes him as happy as it has made me, then he will soon be well again."

Sing Little Birdie

DOUGAL and Brian were coming to tea, so Florence was very busy in the kitchen making a big red raspberry jelly. "M-m-m-m—how delicious that looks," she thought as she carefully placed fruit and sweets around the bottom of the jelly. Raspberry jelly was one of Dougal's favourite things, so she knew that he would be pleased. She was about to start preparing the cucumber sandwiches when she noticed a little bird fly through the open window. It was flying so fast that it nearly flew into the middle of the jelly.

"What a delightful little bird," said Florence. "Its feathers are all yellow and blue. She must be a very happy little bird because she is singing such a fine song."

Florence was wrong, however, for although the little bird was singing, she noticed that it was also crying, and tears ran like small rivers down its tiny cheeks.

"Why are you crying?" asked Florence.

"I cannot stop singing," sang the little bird.

"Fine song! Fine song!" said Dougal, popping his big black nose around the door.

"Happy song! Happy song!" said Brian, as he peered in through the open window.

Dougal and Brian were soon to stop smiling when Florence told them all about the unhappy little bird.

"What can we do to help?" asked Brian.

All three then sat down upon the floor and started to think of ways to help the unhappy little bird.

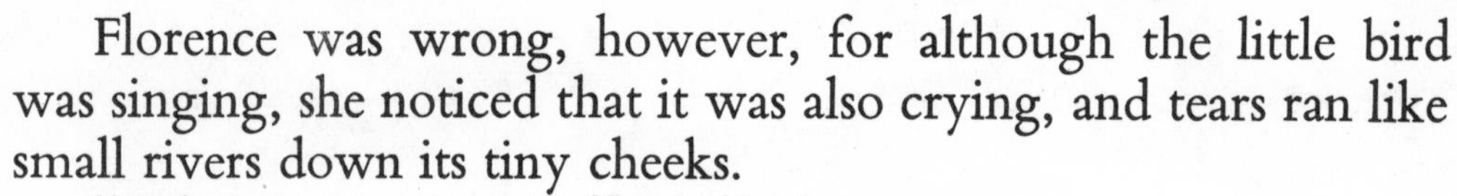

"We shall go and see Dr. Curem," said Dougal after a little while. "Oh, what a splendid idea, Dougal," said Florence.

Dr. Curem lived in a small cottage on the edge of the village green. It was a pretty little cottage with old green beams. It was surrounded by cherry and plum trees, and the garden was filled with sweet-smelling flowers of every colour.

Florence put the little bird into a golden

cage. Then they all made their way across the green to the house of Dr. Curem.

"The cure is simple," said Dr. Curem, when he was told about the unhappy little bird, and he gave Florence a small piece of red ribbon to tie around its neck.

"When you untie the ribbon, it will release the song," said Dr. Curem smiling.

Florence tied the ribbon in a tiny bow and instantly the singing stopped, and instead of crying the little bird was laughing happily as she flew into the air.

Florence, Dougal and Brian then hurried back home where they knew platefuls of lovely sandwiches and raspberry jelly awaited them.

If you ever see a little blue and yellow bird with a red ribbon tied round its neck, you will be able to tell your friends all about it, won't you!

TO CATCH A BUTTERFLY

THE cool water rippled over the white pebbles of Bramble Brook. Dylan sat in the shade of an old willow tree lazily strumming his guitar. The morning sun was hot and Dylan drowsily began to sing to himself.

"I sit all day and play and
play,
I'll sing my song all day
long."

Whilst Dylan was singing to himself he noticed a white shape disappear behind the holly hedge. Dylan rose lazily to his feet and slowly went to investigate. At the other side of the hedge what do you think he found? There was Basil with a huge white net, trying to catch a large blue butterfly as it fluttered from flower to flower.

"What on earth are you doing, Basil?" asked Dylan.

"I'm trying to catch a butterfly for Rosalie," said Basil. "She wants to take it to school for her nature study lesson.

"I have been chasing this butterfly all morning, and I simply cannot catch it," said Basil breathlessly.

"I don't think that you will ever catch it," Dylan remarked. "It's much quicker than you are. I think I shall have to help you."

Basil would creep up slowly behind the butterfly, but just as he was about to catch it, the butterfly would flutter up into the air, just out of reach of Basil's net.

Dylan could do no better, for he kept falling over on his face and frightening the butterfly away.

From harebell to buttercup, from dandelion to mayflower she fluttered, always too smart for the two eager chasers. Over the stile, over the hawthorn tree, over the brook and up into the blue sky fluttered the butterfly.

Basil and Dylan chased the butterfly until they could run no further, but always the butterfly was just out of reach, and in the end collapsed on the grass quite worn out.

"That butterfly's too clever for us, Dylan," said Basil rather breathlessly.

"Yeh," said Dylan in his usual drawly voice, and he lay back and closed his eyes.

"I'm afraid Rosalie will have to go to her nature lesson without a butterfly," went on Basil.

"Hmm," said Dylan, which did not mean anything much—only that he was feeling rather sleepy.

So Basil gave

up trying to talk to him. And after laying down beside Dylan, they were soon both fast asleep.

Basil was the first to wake up. The sun was lower now—only just above the top of Mr. MacHenry's lemon tree.

"It must be nearly tea time," thought Basil.

He turned to Dylan, who was still fast asleep and dreaming of lettuces.

"Wake up, Dylan," he said. "It's tea time."

Dylan woke up. He yawned, stretched, slowly got to his

feet, picked up his guitar and hurriedly joined Basil, who was already on his way home.

They hadn't gone very far when Dylan's guitar began to play.

"That's a fine tune you are playing," said Basil.

"But *I'm* not playing," said Dylan, looking very surprised.

They both looked at the guitar—and what do you think they found there? The beautiful blue butterfly they'd tried so very hard to catch was tiptoeing across the strings of Dylan's guitar and playing them a lovely tune. Dylan had never heard anything so lovely.

Rosalie saw the butterfly and hugged Basil and Dylan in her delight.

All the school children cheered when they heard its beautiful music.

a day in the park

DOUGAL, Paul and Zebedee
once in the park did play.
They sailed their boats and flew
their kites—
It was such a lovely day.
They swung on the swings and slid
down the slide—
And the roundabouts were fine.

They sat and played with their buckets and
spades,
And had a splendid time.
With a beach ball they played and drank
lemonade,
And were very happy to see,
Florence, Brian and Rosalie having a picnic
tea.
"Come and have some tea," said Rosalie,
And they ate till nearly dark.
Then home to their beds to rest
their heads
After a wonderful day in
the park.

DOUGAL to the RESCUE

MR. SCAREM is a scarecrow who lives in the corner of a large cornfield at the edge of the Magic Village. He is a jolly person with a large green hat, a red jacket and blue trousers. Round his neck is a smart check scarf of which he is very proud. He stands happily in the cornfield frightening all the naughty birds that come to steal the corn.

Florence and Dougal had been shopping and were on their way home.

"Good morning, Mr. Scarem," said Florence.

"Lovely morning," said Dougal happily. But Mr. Scarem said nothing.

"Why are you unhappy?" asked Florence. "Are you ill?"

"No, I am not ill," said Mr. Scarem, "but I no longer scare the crows and the naughty birds are stealing all the corn."

"We shall have to put a stop to that," said Dougal.

"Don't worry, Mr. Scarem," said Florence.

Dougal rushed over to the shopping bag and started to open all the cans of food that they had bought that morning. When he had emptied all the cans of food, he tied them together with a long piece of string and then tied the cans to the end of Mr. Scarem's wooden arms. When the wind blew

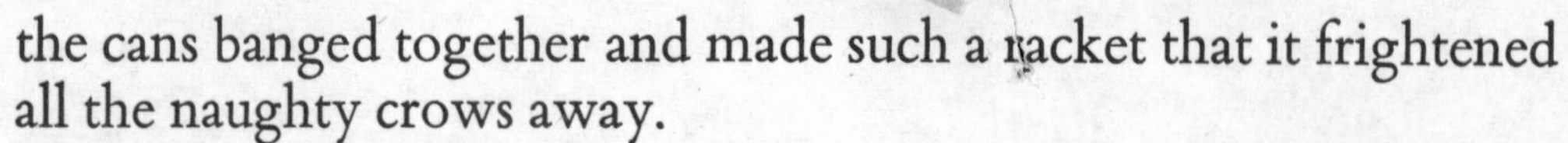

the cans banged together and made such a racket that it frightened all the naughty crows away.

"I don't think they will bother you again," said Dougal.

"I'm the happiest scarecrow in the world," said Mr. Scarem. "But what about all the wasted food?"

"Not to worry," Dougal replied. "It was worth it to see you happy once again."

"Come along, Dougal," said Florence. "I think we have some more shopping to do!"